D1326000

The Witches' Party
and other scary stories

The Witches' Party
and other scary stories

Written by
Caroline Repchuk and Geoff Cowan

Illustrated by
Diana Catchpole, Chris Forsey and
Claire Mumford

p

This is a Parragon Book
This edition published in 2001

Parragon
Queen Street House
4 Queen Street
Bath BA1 1HE, UK

Produced by
The Templar Company plc.

Copyright © Parragon 2000
This material has previously been published in *Spooky Stories*,
published 1999

Printed and bound in China
ISBN 0 75255 684 3

Contents

OCTOBER

S M T W T F
1 2 3 4
5 6 7 8 9 10 11
12 13 14 15 16 17 18
19 20 21 22 23 24 25
26 27 28 29 30 31

The Witches' Party

I t's almost Halloween again," said Snitchy
Witch to her black cat Treacle. "How the time
has flown! And I still haven't quite finished
making the food for the Witches Convention.
I must do it today."

So she sat down at the table and started to write
her shopping list which went something like this:
2 newts; 3 frogs; bag of snails; tin of slug juice;
1 rat's tail; packet of mixed spiders... She was so
busy writing that she didn't notice the little ghost
watching her carefully from behind the cauldron...

Now, Halloween, as you all know, is a very special time for witches, and this witch was no exception. In fact, this Halloween was *extra* special for Snitchy Witch as she was hosting the WESTERN WITCHES ANNUAL HALLOWEEN CONVENTION. She was holding it in the ballroom of the Haunted House, hired specially for the occasion. Witches were coming from far and wide to attend lectures on important topics, such as *Magic Brooms and How to Handle Them*; *Growing Warts in a Week* and *If you Want to Get Ahead, Get a Cat!*

The highlight of the event would be a *Spelling Contest,* where the witches would compete for the coveted title of WITCH OF THE YEAR.

"Just wait until it's my turn," said Snitchy Witch as she finished her list. "I'll show 'em a thing or two!" and she hurried off on her broomstick to the shops.

As soon as he was sure she had gone, Spooky, the little ghost, came out from behind the cauldron. He didn't like stinky witches. Having just one in the Haunted House was bad enough — but a whole convention! It was no use trying to frighten them away — witches weren't afraid of a little ghost like him. But perhaps there was a way to make them scare themselves… Spooky smiled. He would certainly have some fun with those silly old witches…

Snitchy Witch returned from her shopping expedition and spent the rest of the day carefully cooking up the most disgusting food she could think of. Then she dusted off her spellbook and polished up her favourite magic wand. She could hardly wait to demonstrate her spectacular 'garden slug into gigantic gooey chocolate cake' spell! And all the time she was busy preparing, Spooky was busy watching her…

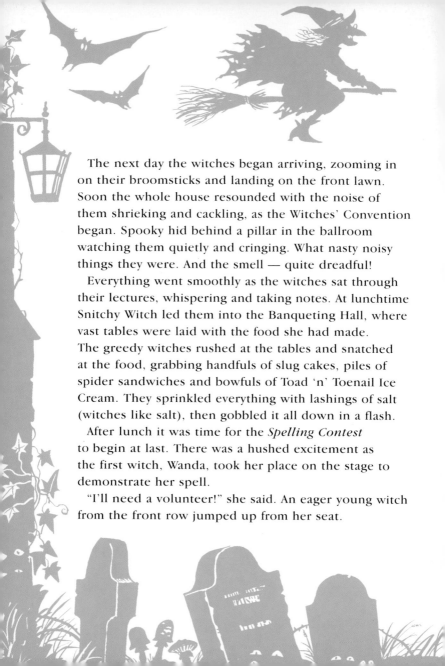

The next day the witches began arriving, zooming in on their broomsticks and landing on the front lawn. Soon the whole house resounded with the noise of them shrieking and cackling, as the Witches' Convention began. Spooky hid behind a pillar in the ballroom watching them quietly and cringing. What nasty noisy things they were. And the smell — quite dreadful!

Everything went smoothly as the witches sat through their lectures, whispering and taking notes. At lunchtime Snitchy Witch led them into the Banqueting Hall, where vast tables were laid with the food she had made. The greedy witches rushed at the tables and snatched at the food, grabbing handfuls of slug cakes, piles of spider sandwiches and bowfuls of Toad 'n' Toenail Ice Cream. They sprinkled everything with lashings of salt (witches like salt), then gobbled it all down in a flash.

After lunch it was time for the *Spelling Contest* to begin at last. There was a hushed excitement as the first witch, Wanda, took her place on the stage to demonstrate her spell.

"I'll need a volunteer!" she said. An eager young witch from the front row jumped up from her seat.

"You're in for a treat!" said Wanda. "I'm going to turn you into a stinking sewer rat! Just temporarily, of course."

"Ooh, lovely," said the young volunteer. "What fun."

Wanda raised her arms, waved her magic wand, and muttered the magic spell:

"She's not the last, she'll be the first, come mystic magic, do your worst!"

The witches watched in eager anticipation, as with a loud bang, a great flash, and a crackle of sparks the volunteer witch transformed before their eyes. But what was this? Instead of becoming a stinking rat, she had changed into a beautiful princess! Wanda looked at her in horror. There's absolutely

nothing witches hate more than beautiful princesses — what a nightmare!

"Boo!" jeered the witches. "You're rubbish! Get that disgusting princess thing out of here!"

"What's the matter?" asked the princess, who could not see herself, and didn't know what all the fuss was about. Wanda held up a mirror.

"Aargh!" yelled the princess and fled from the room, screaming. But in the next moment there was a great eruption of bangs and flashes, whizzes and whirls, as all over the room the witches transformed one by one, until the whole room was filled with lovely princesses.

Then, what a fuss and commotion! They hollered and screamed and jumped up and down, clutching at their shiny hair and beautiful gowns. Spooky laughed and laughed until he cried, for of course the commotion was all his fault. He had made a spell for beautiful princesses which he had found at the back of Snitchy Witch's spell book while she was out shopping. "Only to be used on your worst enemies, or in emergencies," it had said. Spooky decided this was definitely an emergency, and had added the spell to the salt (which, as you remember, the witches had used plenty of on their lunch!).

Still yelling and screaming (most unladylike!) the princesses leapt on their brooms and fled.

"Come back!" yelled Snitchy Witch (now transformed into a princess herself). "We haven't finished the contest!" But it was no use. The witches, or rather princesses, had gone. Spooky stretched out on an old sofa with a satisfied grin on his face. Peace and quiet once more. Only one stinky witch left in the Haunted House, and even she wasn't too bad now she was a princess!

Welcome to the Haunted House!

Step in through the rusty gates —
Be quiet as a mouse.
We're going to sneak, and take
a peek, inside the Haunted House!

Ghosts are hooting in the hallway.
Ghastly ghouls lurk on the stairs.
Imps and sprites have pillow fights
to catch you unawares!

In the kitchen there's a wizard,
making slug and spider pies.
They're for a very special meal —
A Halloween surprise!

Upstairs in the dusty bedrooms
skeletons are getting dressed.
Vampires brush their hair and teeth.
All the spooks must look their best!

An empty suit of shiny armour
is clanking loudly down the hall,
to a party in the ballroom —
It's the Monster's Secret Ball!

So while the party's in full swing,
be quiet as a mouse.
Tiptoe out while you still can —
Escape the Haunted House!

The Hungry Ghost

Becky had just sat down to have breakfast (scrambled eggs and bacon), when something very strange happened. The salt and pepper pots rose up from the table and floated through the air towards her father's plate, where his breakfast sat waiting for him to appear. Becky's jaw dropped open in surprise.

"Mum!" she called to her mother.
"The pepper pot's floating in mid-air!"

"Very nice, darling," called her mum, who
was watching breakfast television and not
paying attention.

Becky looked back at the table. There, in her
father's chair, sat a little ghost with a napkin
around his neck, holding a knife and fork.
He was tucking into her father's breakfast.

"Very good!" said the ghost. "Bacon's a bit
salty, mind you!"

Becky could not believe her eyes!

"Mum!" she shouted. "Look! There's a ghost
eating Daddy's breakfast!"

"What's that? More toast for breakfast?"
called her mum, distractedly. "Just coming!"

The hungry little ghost gobbled his way
through the scrambled eggs and three slices

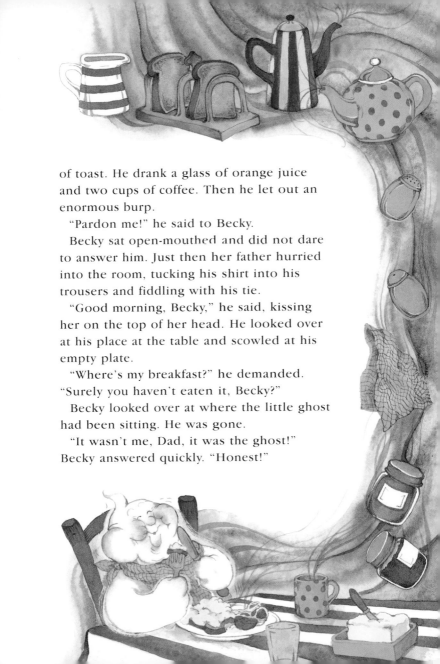

of toast. He drank a glass of orange juice and two cups of coffee. Then he let out an enormous burp.

"Pardon me!" he said to Becky.

Becky sat open-mouthed and did not dare to answer him. Just then her father hurried into the room, tucking his shirt into his trousers and fiddling with his tie.

"Good morning, Becky," he said, kissing her on the top of her head. He looked over at his place at the table and scowled at his empty plate.

"Where's my breakfast?" he demanded. "Surely you haven't eaten it, Becky?"

Becky looked over at where the little ghost had been sitting. He was gone.

"It wasn't me, Dad, it was the ghost!" Becky answered quickly. "Honest!"

"Ghost? Don't be ridiculous, there are no such things as ghosts!" said her dad, impatiently.

"But there was, Dad. He was sitting right there in your chair. He even used your napkin!" Becky protested, pointing to the screwed-up napkin.

"Becky, I don't have time for this nonsense. I'm late for work!" said her father, crossly. "Sandra, where's my breakfast gone?" he called to his wife. Becky's mum came in, and blinked in astonishment when she saw the empty plate.

"I put it right there," she said in amazement. "Becky can't have eaten yours *and* hers!"

"I didn't," Becky protested. "It was the ghost!"

"Oh, really, Becky! I've had enough of this. Go to your room!" snapped her father.

Becky stood up to do as she was told. But as she did so, she caught sight of the armchair and smiled. "Well, if you don't believe me, look behind you," she said.

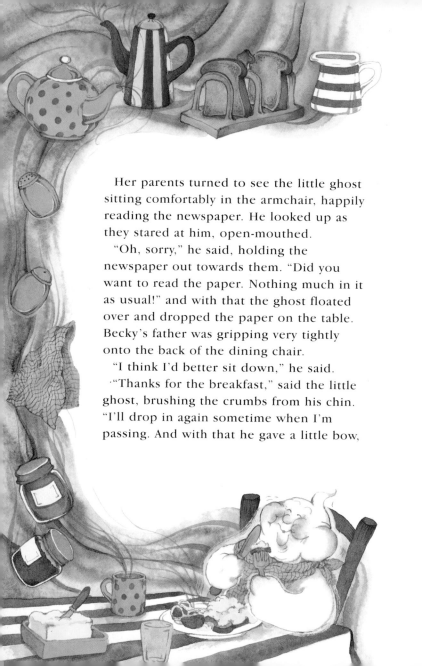

Her parents turned to see the little ghost sitting comfortably in the armchair, happily reading the newspaper. He looked up as they stared at him, open-mouthed.

"Oh, sorry," he said, holding the newspaper out towards them. "Did you want to read the paper. Nothing much in it as usual!" and with that the ghost floated over and dropped the paper on the table. Becky's father was gripping very tightly onto the back of the dining chair.

"I think I'd better sit down," he said.

"Thanks for the breakfast," said the little ghost, brushing the crumbs from his chin. "I'll drop in again sometime when I'm passing. And with that he gave a little bow,

and disappeared through the wall.

Becky's dad blinked and rubbed his eyes. He looked at his wife, who simply spread out her hands and shrugged her shoulders. Then he looked at Becky, who was smiling triumphantly.

"I told you," she said. Finally, he looked down at the table and sat staring at the paper in stunned silence.

"I don't believe it!" he said at last, amazed. "He's even finished the crossword!"

Things that go Bump

While you are tucked up, fast asleep,
out from dark corners
strange things creep.

But steady your nerves, don't take fright,
when things go bump in the night!

Ghosts glide down the hallway,
sneak under your bed,
and pull at the pillows
where you rest your head.

But steady your nerves, don't take fright,
when things go bump in the night!

Spooks pull off your blankets.
They tweak at your toes.
They use small white feathers
to tickle your nose.
But steady your nerves, don't take fright,
when things go bump in the night!

Ghouls empty your toybox.
They try on your clothes.
They tie up your teddy
with pink satin bows.

But steady your nerves, don't take fright,
when things go bump in the night!

The ghosts like to feast at the end of your bed.
They leave behind spilt drinks,
and stale crumbs of bread.

But steady your nerves, don't take fright,
when things go bump in the night!

For night-time's the time when
the spooks like to play.
At the first sign of daylight,
they hurry away.
So steady your nerves, don't take fright
When things go bump in the night!

Little Ghost Lost

"Come along, Percy," said Mummy. "It's time we took you out on your first proper spooking expedition. And what better night for spooking than Halloween!" "But what do we actually *do* when we go out spooking?" asked Percy.

"Just follow us and copy what we do and you'll soon find out," said Daddy. "But you must remember to stick close, and don't wander off on your own."

With that, Mr and Mrs Ghost and their young son Percy set off on their first night of spooking together. They floated up through the chimney of their home in the Haunted House, and curled out of the top like whisps of smoke. They hovered over the rooftop, then slunk off into the deep, dark night to see what fun they could have.

At the edge of some woods they came to a little cottage, with a fire glowing brightly inside. An old man was heading down the garden path towards the woodpile.

"Follow me," said Daddy. "This will be fun!"

The family of ghosts hid and watched as the old man piled some logs high in his arms. Then with a terrible wail Mr and Mrs Ghost rose up

from behind the woodpile and the old man leapt in the air in fright, sending the wood flying. He ran back to his cottage hollering and screaming, and the ghosts collapsed in giggles.

"That was brilliant!" said Percy.

Next they came to a house with a pumpkin lantern in the window.

"Looks like these folk are entering into the *spirit* of the evening," laughed Mrs Ghost. Peering in through a steamy window, they saw a woman busy baking pumpkin pie. Mr Ghost tapped on the window, and the woman turned to see three ghostly faces pressed against the glass. She threw her arms up and screamed, knocking over a large bag of flour as she did so. The flour puffed up in a big cloud, smothering the poor woman from head to toe.

"She looks pretty ghostly herself, now!" laughed Percy.

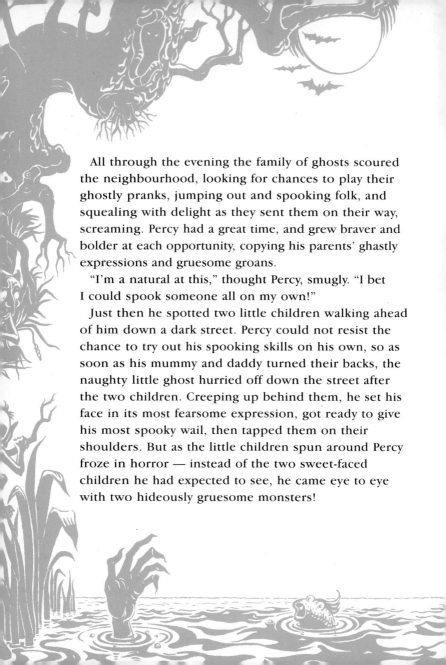

All through the evening the family of ghosts scoured the neighbourhood, looking for chances to play their ghostly pranks, jumping out and spooking folk, and squealing with delight as they sent them on their way, screaming. Percy had a great time, and grew braver and bolder at each opportunity, copying his parents' ghastly expressions and gruesome groans.

"I'm a natural at this," thought Percy, smugly. "I bet I could spook someone all on my own!"

Just then he spotted two little children walking ahead of him down a dark street. Percy could not resist the chance to try out his spooking skills on his own, so as soon as his mummy and daddy turned their backs, the naughty little ghost hurried off down the street after the two children. Creeping up behind them, he set his face in its most fearsome expression, got ready to give his most spooky wail, then tapped them on their shoulders. But as the little children spun around Percy froze in horror — instead of the two sweet-faced children he had expected to see, he came eye to eye with two hideously gruesome monsters!

Percy screeched at the top of his voice and fled into the night. He didn't even hear the screams behind him, or see the monsters run home at top speed, where they tore off their Halloween masks and panted out their story to their mother. Poor Percy had never heard of trick-or-treating!

Percy fled down the streets turning this way and that, calling for his mother and father. Where had he left them? He had never been out on his own before, and now all the streets looked the same. Suddenly he felt afraid of the dark. Sinister shadows lurched at him, trees clutched at him with spiky fingers and strange furry monsters hissed at him and swiped him with sharp claws. Poor Percy hurried on through the night — but tonight was the night when witches, wizards, monsters

and ghouls were abroad, and at every turn fresh horrors awaited him. Finally he sank exhausted into a doorway.

"I want my mummy!" he wailed, and began to cry. Before very long he had cried himself to sleep. Hours later he woke with a start. Something was poking and prodding him with a sharp stick.

"What have we here then?" said a mean little voice.

"Looks like a wee ghostie — we can have some fun with him. Let's pinch him!" said another nasty voice. The voices belonged to two goblins — mean, dirty, smelly little goblins, with sharp noses, pointed ears and bony fingers.

"BOO!" said Percy, pulling his most gruesome face. "Leave me alone!"

But the goblins just collapsed in a fit of giggles — it takes a lot to frighten goblins.

"Is that the best you can do?" they taunted and started to poke and pinch poor Percy again. He howled and wailed and pulled all manner of fearsome faces, trying to scare the goblins away, but it just made them laugh all the more and pinch him even harder.

"You can't scare us!" they teased. "Nothing scares us!"

"Oh no?" said a deep voice behind them "How about this!"

The little goblins turned to see two enormous, terrifying ghosts hovering over them ready to pounce. "Help!" they cried as they ran into the night!

"Mummy! Daddy!" cried Percy in delight. "You found me!"

Soon the ghost family were safely back
in the Haunted House, and Mrs Ghost was
tucking Percy into bed.

"I'm never going to make a good spook!"
said Percy miserably.

"Yes you will," soothed Mummy. "After all,
you certainly managed to scare us! We were
very worried about you. Next time remember
to stick close!"

"I promise," said Percy, and in no time at
all he was sound asleep, dreaming of ways
to spook goblins.

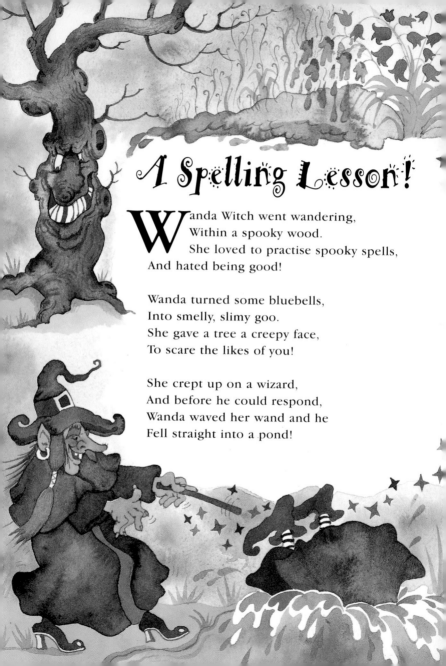

A Spelling Lesson!

Wanda Witch went wandering,
Within a spooky wood.
She loved to practise spooky spells,
And hated being good!

Wanda turned some bluebells,
Into smelly, slimy goo.
She gave a tree a creepy face,
To scare the likes of you!

She crept up on a wizard,
And before he could respond,
Wanda waved her wand and he
Fell straight into a pond!

Although it was not very deep,
The wizard soon saw red.
He cast a spell which made his cloak,
Flap right round Wanda's head.

It wrapped around her body,
And squeezed her really tight.
"Say sorry," roared the wizard,
"Or stay like that all night!"

The witch agreed and told him,
"Your magic is so fast.
No more naughty spells from me,
I've really cast my last!"